I0692285

# Madison's Christmas

SAMANTHA GOLLAKNER

ISBN:
978-0-9983459-9-4

# DEDICATION

We may not always be together,
but you are always on my mind
and there will forever be a special
place in my heart just for you.
I love you, honey.
Merry Christmas, Madison.
Love always, Auntie Sam

There is a Fairy named Madison, who lives deep in the magical forest of Star Dust Peak. It is not found on any map or even in the deepest of crevasses or creeks, but I promise you one thing, it is real. This I know for a fact. Madison is an only child, living with her mother, father and grandmother. They live in the biggest tree in the forest and eat only the best of meals. Madison was raised to be perfect. She was told all the time that in order to be happy, she had to fit in and be like everyone else, but every single word that ever left her father's mouth hung heavy along her heart. She could not help but notice that she did not want to be the same. She was different than the rest of the kids and the only one who she could be herself around was her grandmother. This feeling in her heart started from a very early age, but it had grown heavier one night when her father, mother and grandmother were all sitting down to enjoy a lovely dinner of strawberry, milk, honey and cinnamon soup. It was just like any other night when her mother and father talked about work, bills and money.

However, her grandmother changed the mood fast as she nudged Madison's arm with hers, "Do you want to hear a story?"

Before Madison has a chance to answer, her father has already made up her mind for her, speaking in a harsh tone, "She does not want to hear any story coming from you, they are all nonsense, Mom. All you are doing is filling her head with stuff she has no need to know."

Madison can feel the anger bubbling inside of her chest, "No, I want to hear the story."

The realization of what she had just done causes all of the color to drain from her face. Her grandmother quickly begins dripping words from her lips to avoid an unnecessary spat, "A very long time ago when I was young, I was quite rebellious and when everyone in Star Dust Peak was sleeping, I went out to find an adventure of my own. I had traveled not too far, before I ran into some humans. I overheard them talking among one another about a man named Santa Claus. From what I was able to gather from their conversation he was tall, chubby and jolly. He wears long, white beard and funny, red clothes. He travels all over the world in just one night to bring presents to all of the children in the world making certain, that not even one would awake on Christmas morning without a present under their tree."

1

Madison's eyes sparkle and glow as she listens to the story, her mouth twitches as if she has just become puzzled, "How does he do that?"

Her grandmother laughs loudly, "Christmas Magic I suppose, my dear."

Madison has a hint of confusion lining her next statement, "I thought we were the only ones with magic."

Her grandmother lightly touches her hand, "Well, then I guess, you are just going to have to go to the North Pole and ask him yourself!"

Her father slams his right palm along the surface of the table, "I told you a million times not to tell her stories like that! You never listen to me, and neither do you Madison. How many times do I have to tell you, do not listen to your grandmother! She has no idea what she is talking about, she does not know anything! Now, go get ready for bed, you have school tomorrow."

Madison huffs, sliding out of the chair, gently kissing her grandmother on the cheek before running off to bed. While Madison is brushing her teeth, she overhears her father and grandmother talking in the kitchen.

Her father growls, "I cannot have you filling her head with lies. She cannot be going around believing in Santa Claus, when he does not exist. You have no idea how this is going to affect her or me."

Her grandmother rolls her eyes, "What is so wrong with a little girl having dreams and something to believe in?"

Her father crosses his arms tightly over the surface of his chest, "This is not going to end well, you will see. Things in her life will only work out if she just fits in and acts like everyone else. Do you want the other children to think that she is crazy? Do you want them to laugh at her? Keep it up, Mom. Then when she is hurt, you will have to deal with it."

Madison gasps hearing their conversation. She does not understand how her father can be so cruel to her grandmother. She drags herself into bed with a heavy sorrow hanging over her heart. The next day, Madison finds herself sluggishly getting ready. She sits in front of the mirror, using the gentle stroke of a tree branch to comb through her long, beautiful, blonde hair. She splashes some water onto the pale surface of her face, washing the dust from last night's dreams free from her sparkling, blue eyes. Her right hand reaches across the abstract sink to grab her toothbrush, crafted from a wooden branch. With every movement, her ice blue wings flutter gracefully behind her. She stands only a mere three-inches tall. Her small figure effortlessly glides from room to room. Her father is in the kitchen looking out the window, lost in a mindless daydream. He stands at a height of five-inches, running his fingers through his short, brown hair. The morning sun awakens inside the glistening hue of his blue-green eyes, the leaves of one of his older suits, crinkle and crack with every movement. His strong, dark blue wings do not show the same grace as his daughter's. His are full of wisdom which he keeps held high with pride as he awaits patiently for Madison, who is just now walking into the kitchen. She kisses her mother, who has long, blonde hair and olive-green eyes, her body is wrapped in a tree bark dress, sprinkled with daisy flower petals for a unique finish. Madison then makes her way over towards her grandmother, who has her gray hair tide up in a messy bun on the top of her head, held in place with twigs. Loose strands of her hair fall along the shoulders of her dress which is crafted from gray, bird feathers that ignite her deep blue eyes to a comforting glow.

She turns towards her father, "I am ready, when you are."

5

They are blinded by the morning sun dancing over the horizon in the near distance as they step out into the wide, open space of the city. Every step away from the front door, pulls the sun out of view allowing them to get a clear visual of the surroundings. Their glossy vision comes to life with fairies young and old, flying high in the sky while playing in the drips of dew running along the surface of the grass blades. It does not take them long to take their travel to the sky as well. Madison peers around at the river that gently flows through the city, running on auto-pilot. Their landing is soft. The sight of Madison's friends in the distance causes her breath to catch hard in her throat, she runs off to greet them by the entrance. Her father exhales a deep breath of sorrow, watching her run off without even the slightest acknowledgement of their parting. The strands of her wavy locks, flow in a backwards movement as the stride of her legs begin to pick up pace. The bright glow of her wings disappears into the darkness that surrounds the school's entrance which is tucked safely away inside of the inner makings of a large, oak tree. He can do nothing in this moment, but watch her slip further and further away from his grasp.

Once Madison finally gets settled down in class, her teacher, Mrs. Sparks walks in. Her long, deep brown hair is held up loosely inside of a calming bun. Untamed strands brush along the red rose petals that construct her dress which is wrapped tightly along her small figure. She would appear to be prepared for work as usual, never letting the fragments of the outside world interfere with her job position. Madison becomes captivated by the knock of her heels clinking along the wooden surface of the floor. When she finally arrives at the front of the class, she greets the children with a warming smile. She loudly clasping her hands together to get everyone's attention, "Okay, kids! I hope everyone remembers what today is! It is the annual fifth-grade show and tell day here in Star Dust Peak! Who would like to go first? Any volunteers?"

Her smile begins to slightly drain from her face as she peers around the class, seeing that no one is raising their hand to take the courageous step of going first.

Mrs. Sparks shakes her head slightly, releasing a small chuckle, "Well, since no one wants to pick for themselves then I guess, I am going to have to choose. Hmm. How about Madison? Come on, Madison. How about it? Show the class what you brought!"

All of the sudden, Madison feels the pressure of everyone staring at her, she begins to fire up inside with fear as she slowly stands up. Her timid legs carry the jelly-like substance of her shaken body towards the front of the class. The upper lining of her cheeks burns with a bright red as a shaken, vocal breaks from her lips, "Uh. Well, you see I do not have a thing to show, but I do have something to tell. There is an amazing guy named Santa Claus. On Christmas Eve, he breaks into people's houses and leaves presents under big, pine trees in their living room that the humans call a Christmas tree. He travels around the world in just one night with flying reindeer which are like big dogs. He goes through all of that trouble just to make sure that not one child will wake up on Christmas morning without a present under their tree."

The whole class stares at Madison blankly in silence, trying to wrap their minds around the magical world that Madison just introduced to them.

9

One girl, named Erin Clouds stands up, pulling all of the attention on to herself, releasing a harsh laugh, "Mrs. Sparks. Please, correct me if I am wrong, but wasn't the topic show and tell, not show and tale? Since Madison misunderstood the whole project, I think my fellow classmates and I will all agree that she should be failed for the little show she just put on. Wouldn't you?"

Mrs. Sparks looks the girl up and down, noticing her fancy, tree bark dress and the set of small gems that are entangled in her hair. Upon her observation of the source of information, she has a hard time holding in a slight chuckle, "Miss Clouds, I do believe that I am the teacher and it is my choice whether I personally believe if Madison should be failed or not. Although, Madison did not seem to grasp the purpose of the project assigned, she did tell an amazing story that must have taken a lot of time and effort to establish. For that, I think it is fair to give her at least a C+."

Madison tips her head forward, dragging her body back towards her seat. She quickly dumps her weight into the chair, hiding her face in the crossed folds of her arms, remaining perfectly still for the rest of the day.

The loud blare of the bell sends a shiver down her spine, giving the rest of the children the okay to leave for the day. They waste no time flooding out of the classroom and into the halls, nearly knocking themselves and others down to the ground in the mess. Madison stays out of the crowd and waits for everything to calm down before she even tries to get out of the school. Once she thinks the coast is clear, she peeks her head around the door frame, not wanting to face anyone right now. She takes a deep breath, not seeing a soul in sight, she begins venturing down the hallway. She hopes that everyone has by now long forgotten all about her story regarding Santa Claus.

She is greeted by other kids in the hallway who are whispering, pointing and laughing at her as she rushes past them to advance out of the school doors. She takes a deep inhale of fresh air, the flooding feeling of relief flushes over her face to be free from the bullying. Her eyes scan along the crowd of people outside of the structure to see her father, who is waiting to greet her and hear about her day, just as he always is every time. Her father can tell right away by the look on her face that something is bothering her, not to mention, she did not greet him with her normal huge, warm hug. He places his hand on her back in a guiding gesture as they begin to walk home, "What is the matter, sweetheart? Please, tell me what is bothering you."

You can see in her eyes that she wanted nothing more than for him to have never asked. She does not want to tell him, knowing how he will react when he hears the truth, but deep in her heart she knows she cannot lie to him. She takes a deep breath, "I got made fun of today by the whole class. Everyone laughed at me and I got a C on my project."

Her father's jaw line tightens, it is clear he is not happy at all to hear this, "Why? Why would anyone make fun of you?"

Madison speaks in almost an invisible whisper, "Well, I told them the story of Santa Claus and I guess, nobody believed me."

Her father straightens his back slightly, "I will just have to talk to your grandmother about this tonight when we get home. For now, do not let it get to you. I will make sure this will never happen to you again. As for what happened today, kids will find something better to make fun of tomorrow and your story will be long forgotten."

They enter their house moments later, not giving her father even the slightest chance to calm down. His eyes dart around the area, speaking to Madison in a stern, indirect manner, "Go to your room, honey. Grandma and I need to have a grown-up conversation."

Madison does as her father says, but listens by the door of her bedroom. She overhears her father's stern tone blow through the wooden door, "Okay, we have to talk. This is very serious. This thing with Santa Claus and all of these make-believe stories have to stop. I told you just last night that this would affect Madison and now it has. She got made fun of by everyone in school today and her teacher failed her for using the story you told her as a project idea for show and tell."

The innocent flow of her grandmother's voice is calming to her hectic brain, "Kids have to fight for what they believe in, even if she stands alone; at least she is standing up for something good. It is not my fault that no one here has any sense of magic other than what they see every day. Just because they do not believe in it, does not mean that it is not true."

Her father slams his right foot along the surface of the flooring panels, "I am sorry, but unless you give her something to believe in that is real, I cannot allow you to keep getting her hopes up towards things that will never happen. Unless you can bring Santa Claus here, then I am sorry but you are going to have to leave. I cannot have my daughter's life ruined over a fairy tale."

An underline of pain floods her grandmother's tone, "If that is how you feel, fine. I understand."

When Madison hears the ending of the conversation, she knows she has to do something, anything she possibly can to save her grandmother and prove that she was in fact telling the truth. She knows that this would be the only way to make her father believe that her grandmother would never do anything to harm her. When Madison is crawling into bed, she looks out her window, staring up at the stars, not feeling even the slightest bit of tiredness in her soul. It would feel to her like she has been lying in bed for hours alone, in the dark. She slowly and quietly creeps out into the living room, making sure everyone is asleep. Once she is sure nobody will catch her, she returns back into her bedroom and looks out into the night sky once more while thinking to herself, *'I know you are real. I know you are out there somewhere. I know you will help me get my father to believe. I just have to find you.'*

15

Madison inhales a deep breath, using all of the strength in her form to slide open her window. She places her right foot in the seal allowing her to jump out of the confines of her bedroom, flying as high as she can into the night sky. She does not take a second look back. At this point, she knows she has already gone too far and there would be severe consequences no matter, so she might as well make her punishment worth it by saving the one person who means the entire world to her.

It does not take long for her to realize that as she is flying over new lands, she begins to feel free. She knows she has to make her journey quick and try to get back as soon as possible, hopefully before the rest of her family members awake in the dawn. She suddenly feels a chilly wind blowing against her skin, carrying with it a new feeling she has never felt before—the cold. At first, she likes this new feeling. It gives her a new sense of happiness, a chance to take in crisp, fresh air as it blows against her face. She is beginning to get used to this new feeling, but her blood is getting colder and colder the further she travels. She notices that the faster she flies, the warmer she feels. She pushes her head down slightly, hoping to increase the speed of her pace, when something zooms past the corner of her vision. This falling unknown causes her mind to automatically bring her body to a halt allowing her to hover in mid-air, giving her a chance to get a better look at what is happening around her. She squints her eyes sharply, seeing that they are clear and wet to the touch as they brush against her pale skin. She can feel a heavy weight laying her in bottom lip when she notices that there are thousands of these things floating all around her. She takes a closer look, noticing that they are all different. Some have shapes in the middle such as circles and triangles while others have swirls. Some that look like a spider has just woven them before her eyes. She is so amazed by these objects, not understanding why they are here. Her curiosity begins to get the best of her and she decides to follow them to see where they are going. Her heart begins to race and the cold seems to not bother her as much now that her excitement begins to fill her soul as her focus is now upon the snowflakes. She follows one that catches her eye over the rest, it has a heart shape in the center that spirals out towards the edges. The faster gravity pulls the tiny snowflake to the ground, the faster Madison flies after it.

She does not even realize how fast she is going before—bash! She slams head first into a huge, snow drift. She does not know what is going on. The constant snow flurries begin to pile on top of her wings, weighing them down leaving her unable to fly. With the weight on her wings, she cannot move at all, even when she uses all of her strength she only keeps falling down. She knows at this point she is done and cannot go on by herself. All she can think is, '*Who is ever going to help me now?*'

An elf appears, wearing a red beanie hat with bells and a mistletoe hanging off the tip. The hat gently brushes along a green, velvet shirt, paired with white, velvet pants draping over his black shoes which are tied to two pieces of wood. They are supposed to be helping him from slipping in the slick conditions while walking through the harsh winter to run some errands for Santa Claus. His eyes catch against something that he finds to be rather funny sticking out of the snow ahead. He walks closer, leaning his weight in a forward motion allowing his right hand to dig under the object sticking out of the ground. He quickly retrieves his hand from the snow to see that inside his palm is a tiny girl. He does not know how long she has been laying in the snow, but he does know that she has to get into some place warm before it is too late. He puts the tiny girl inside of his coat pocket and begins to run as fast as he can back to the North pole. He knows in his heart that Santa Claus will know what to do, he always does.

20

Finally, the two of them have arrived at the North Pole. The elf wastes no time, he quickly runs into the toy workshop and into Santa's office. He lays her down on his desk and wraps her in blankets. When he is done, Santa comes into the office to see Madison laying on the desk, he whispers in the elf's ear, "Come out into the hallway, now."

Once in the hallway, Santa asks the elf, "What is the meaning of this? Why is she here? You know that no outsiders are ever allowed here. Where did you find her?"

The elf replies, "I am so sorry, sir. I understand the rules and I know that you are angry, but she was going to freeze to death. I found her in the snow all alone."

Santa replies, "So, you are telling me that you know nothing about this girl?"

The elf thinks for a minute, "Nope not a thing. What do you want me to do with her, sir?"

Santa strokes his beard with his right hand while rubbing his stomach with his left, "Well, we cannot just let her go outside. So, watch her and when she wakes up, find out everything you can about her then report back to me. We will figure out what to do then. I am going to go find Mrs. Claus and have her make me some milk and cookies, that always calms me down."

The elf nods, "Yes, sir."

He walks back into the office as he shuts the door. It rings with a loud bang that awakens Madison.

Madison slowly begins to shift her eyes open and closed in a fluttering motion, when the blurred image of a man fills her vision. With her sight now beginning to focus, a loud scream is forced from her throat, "Who are you and where am I?"

The elf clearly becomes startled, "Whoa, whoa. Just calm down, everything is going to be okay. I am not going to hurt you. You are in Santa's workshop and I am Santa's right-hand man. My name is Alex and I found you laying in the snow. I did not want you to get hurt, so I brought you here."

Madison is staring at Alex blankly with her mouth draped open, "What are you?"

Alex smiles gently, "Well, I am an elf." Then he looks at her with squinted vision while rubbing his chin, "What are you? Some sort of doll that Santa messed up on?"

Madison giggles to herself while covering her mouth, "I do not even know what that is, silly. I am a fairy!"

Alex tilts his head slightly to the left, "If you are a fairy then what are you doing here, at the North Pole?"

Madison inhales deeply, "Well, I am from Star Dust Peak and I live with my father, mother and grandmother. We are not supposed to leave, but my grandmother said when she was younger, she left and over heard some humans talking about Santa Claus and Christmas. After hearing this story, I thought that it was just lovely! Anyway, when I went to school, I told my classmates and everyone made fun of me and said I was lying. When my father found out, he told my grandmother she had to leave our home unless she could bring Santa Claus to Star Dust Peak to prove to my father that he is real. So, I snuck out and came to find him to save my grandmother and bring the magic of Christmas to Star Dust Peak."

Alex cannot wipe the grin from his lips, "That is a magical story. I am going to go tell Santa what happened right now, but you have to stay here and please, do not move. I do not know what would happen if the other elves were to find you."

Madison nods her head in agreement and Alex leaves the office in a flash, being in such a rush, he forgot to fully shut the door behind him. Madison cannot take her eyes off of the door, arguing with the voice inside of her head trying to figure out if it would do any harm if she were to take just one, tiny peek outside in the hallway. It does not take her long to come to the conclusion that if it is only for a second, that no one would ever know. Madison slides off the edge of the table allowing her weight to be held in mid-air by her wings which push her forward towards the entrance of the office. It does not take long for her vision to become flooded with hundreds of elves, who are all dressed just like Alex. They are distracted by some form of a craft. It would appear that they are building some form of a toy, in a line where each elf has their own piece of the puzzle to create an overall master piece. They are working at a constant pace, putting something together that appears to be made out of wood while never looking up from their work. It does not take Madison long before she becomes bored by the elves.

She flies around the whole work shop hoping to find something amazing, when she suddenly comes across an open door with a sign that reads, *Do not enter during work season*. Madison has no idea what this sign could mean, but since the door is already open, she feels that it is safe to go inside. It does not take long before she finds big cages with bars lining the front that look like they were built to keep something held inside of them. Without warning, a creature inside of the cage comes into view. At first, she thinks they are fake, until she gets closer noticing that one of them is eating something orange. The creature is gigantic, hairy and has funny things coming out of the top of its head. Above the cage is a sign that reads, *Reindeer Crossing*. Everything is starting to make sense to her now. These must be like the big dogs her grandmother told her about. She wastes no time to fly through the bars to investigate further. The excitement of her finding is so powerful, she breaks out into joy, doing a three-hundred-and-sixty-degree spin in the air in front of the reindeer's face. Her movements are so fast that some of her blue, fairy dust flies off of her and onto him causing him to break out into a sneezing fit. Madison giggles while running her fingers down the side of his face to feel the warm, softness of his fur against her sensitive skin. She falls in love with the reindeer right away. She does not want to leave him, but she also knows that she has to get back to the office before Alex returns. She hurries and flies back through the workshop, making her way into the office. She places herself back on top of the desk, hoping to make it appear as if she has been there the whole time.

Within minutes, she hears voices trailing down the hall, sounding as if they are heading right for her. She hopes in her heart it is Alex and he is bringing Santa Claus with him. Out of the corner of her vision she sees Alex entering the office and Santa is trailing not too far behind.

Alex smiles waving his right hand in a gesture towards Madison, "Santa, this is—uh?" He then smiles nervously at Madison, "What is your name, again?"

She crosses her arms firmly over her chest, "You never asked. It is Madison and you must be Santa?"

Her eyes dart towards the tall, chubby man in the red overalls. He nods gently, "Why yes, little girl. I very much am Santa. Why don't you come over here, you can sit on my lap and tell me what you want for Christmas."

He walks towards his desk, sitting in a large, red, velvet chair. Her eyes follow him closely, they are filled with confusion, "Why would I have to sit on your lap?"

Santa laughs, "Well, all little girls and boys do that when they tell me what they want for Christmas, but you do not have to if you do not want to. Whatever makes you feel comfortable."

Madison smiles nervously, "I think I will just sit right here. Uh. Well, you see I want you to come to Star Dust Peak with me and prove to my father you exist, so he does not kick my grandmother out of our house without anywhere to go."

Santa turns towards his computer and begins typing something in. Then he leans back while he strokes his beard as if he were thinking, "Alex, is it not coming up on the map?"

Alex shrugs, "Sir, it's not on any map."

Santa nods once, "Then where did she come from?"

Alex frowns, "Where she is from, no one believes in Santa Claus. Not enough to make it be known to us, there is only one woman who believes, Madison's Grandmother."

Santa glances down, "Well, that explains why I have never heard of it. If people do not believe then I do not show up."

Madison speaks in a crackling tone, "I believe in you."

Santa smiles, "That is why you were able to find the North Pole. Only someone with the purest of hearts can find it."

Madison giggles, "Does that mean you are going to help me?"

Santa runs his fingers through his beard, "I will. Tomorrow is Christmas Eve. I do not know how we are going to make Star Dust Peak believe by then." Alex smiles, "Well, since Madison and her grandmother believe, is that enough to at least find their home?" Santa exhales, "With Madison here, we should not have any problem finding it, but what if they think I am just a human dressed in a Santa suit that Madison found?" Alex begins racking his mind, "Then I guess, you and I are going to have a long night ahead of us thinking about what we can do." Santa releases a large laugh, "Yes. Well, in the meantime, it is getting late and Madison needs to go to sleep." Madison groans, "Uh, do I have to?" Santa laughs, "Yes, you do. I will send Mrs. Claus in here shortly. We have a big day tomorrow. You will need your rest." He quickly directs his attention towards Alex, "Go get a blanket and pillow then find her a comfortable spot in my office to lay down." Alex nods, "Yes, sir."

A human woman with gray hair tied up in a loose bun, a red, t-shirt and small, round glasses that cover her baby blue eyes walks in. She has red, baggy pants on with rings of fuzzy, white fabric lining the bottom of the pant legs that are covering the top of her black boots. While she walks in, Santa walks out. He gently shuts the door of the office behind him. The woman turns to Madison, "Hello, Madison. My name is Mrs. Claus and I heard it was time for you to go to sleep. Now, where is Alex with those pillows and blankets?" Madison shrugs, "I do not know, he has not come back yet. Do you want me to go looking for him?" Mrs. Claus smirks, "Oh no, dear. That will be fine." She pulls out a big, red, velvet bag from her pant pocket which appears to be empty, she then reaches her whole arm inside of the bag while making a funny face. Finally, she retrieves a big, white pillow and a matching, huge, fluffy blanket. She moves all of the stuff off of Santa's desk and lays down the blanket then folds it in half long ways. She puts the pillow down on one end of the desk, furthest away from the door, "Okay, honey get comfortable." Madison smiles nervously, "These things are huge, I feel like I am going to drown in them." Mrs. Claus laughs, "It is all we have open at the moment, my dear." Madison knew that fighting it would not get her anywhere, so she simply nods in agreement before laying down. Once comfortable, Mrs. Claus begins to cover her up with the blanket, halfway through the motions she pauses sharply, "Oh, I almost forgot the most important part!" Madison sits up to see what she has forgotten. Mrs. Claus then reaches down into her bag and pulls out a plate full of sugar cookies and a glass of milk with a straw and a book.

Madison's eyes get huge as she sees this, "I have never seen food look like that or so big. I have never seen that much milk in my life! How am I supposed to eat and drink all of that?"

Mrs. Claus laughs, "You only eat and drink what you want. Don't you worry, Santa does not waste milk and cookies."

Madison giggles, "What is the other thing you have in your hand?"

Mrs. Claus tilts her head slightly to the right as if in shock, "A book. I will sit in here and read it to you until you fall asleep."

Madison yawns, "I have never heard of it before."

Mrs. Claus smiles, "Well, get you some cookies and take a drink of milk then sit down on your bed and I will read you the story. I think you will love it!"

Madison's eyes get big as she smiles, "I know I will. I love stories, my grandmother tells me them all the time."

While Mrs. Claus begins to read, the warm milk and cookies kick in. Madison yawns a few times before she is no longer able to hold her eyes open, she slowly sinks down into the pillow. Her eyes become heavier as every new word leaves Mrs. Claus' lips. She wants nothing more than to hear the whole story, but her body fights her harder every second. Before she even knows what is happening, she is out like a light, lost in another world.

Madison is awoken by a loud bang. She hurries to her feet as a shot of fear runs along the inside of her body, not knowing what could possibly be going on. Suddenly, she realizes that she has no idea where she is. She takes a deep breath trying to calm herself down as she looks around, when it hits her that she appears to be in some sort of a house. She looks back to the bed she had just gotten out of which has a small mattress just her size with a matching small, fuzzy, pink blanket. A pink canopy hangs over the bed with sparkles and glitter shimmering in the light that is peering in from the window next to the bed. Madison looks out the window, but does not see anything besides a wall. She rushes out of the bedroom, finding that she is surrounded by a hallway, but has no idea where she is heading. Her weight carries her down a plastic flight of stairs allowing her to step foot on the first floor. The first thing her mind recognizes is an entryway into a kitchen. She enters the area to see a small, two-person, wooden table. With every step that brings her closer to the piece of furniture, she notices that there is an unknown man who is sitting at the table, but she is only able to get a glimpse at the back of his form. He has short, brown hair and a blue shirt on. Madison quietly begins to tip-toe up behind him. Halfway through the kitchen she thinks to herself, *'I do not want to scare him.'* She brings her movements to a fast halt, using her voice to reach out to him, "Hello!"

The mystery man does not answer. She yells again in a louder voice, "Hello, who are you?"

Madison waits a moment for a response. When she does not receive one, she feels anger rise inside of her. The lining of her face flushes beet red as she takes a deep breath, clinching her fists by her sides while she stomps her way over to him. Without thinking about her actions, she pushes his arm, "Hey! I was talking to you!"

He falls out of the chair, the sound of his body slamming into the ground frightens Madison. She becomes so fearful, she runs into the other room and hides behind the black, leather couch in the living room. Madison hears a loud banging again, the same sound that had woken her up earlier, the whole house begins to shake in response. Madison flies over to the door, looking in the kitchen as she passes by the entry, to see that the man is still laying on the floor. With her ear now to the front door, she tries to listen to see if she can determine where the sound is coming from. Without warning, the door begins to open fast. Madison has to jump out of the way, before the door crushes her against the wall. She looks around the wooden panel to see who it is, to her surprise she finds Alex. He is crouched down on the ground, looking into the house, he is peering around the room in a frantic search. A look of disappointment scrolls along his face. Just as he is about to get up, Madison pops out from behind the door, "Are you lost?"

Alex smiles, "Nope, just the fairy I was looking for. Santa has a problem and he needs your help. Come on, follow me." Madison flies as fast as she can to keep up with Alex as he weaves in and out of the other elves full speed ahead. He begins to slow down as they pass through a doorway. Madison notices immediately that is the same doorway which she had passed through the night before with the reindeer. She begins to feel excited to see the reindeer again. Once inside the room she sees that Santa and Mrs. Claus are standing outside of one cage staring into the confines. When Madison and Alex arrive, Santa turns towards them, "Madison, how did you like the house we found you?"

Madison laughs nervously, "It was fine, besides the creepy guy. He would not talk to me and when I touched him, he fell to the floor and would not get up. Who is he and what was he doing there?" Santa laughs a loud and jolly hum, "Oh, honey he is not real. He is just a toy doll. One of the elves must have left him in there. I am sorry it gave you a scare."

You can almost see the stress melt away from Madison's face as she lets out a sigh of relief. Santa frowns, "Okay, Madison we have a problem. My lead reindeer won't eat, drink or move and every time we try and go into his cage, he tries to bite us. We think something might be wrong with one of his paws."

Madison frowns, "Oh, no. Okay, Santa what do you need me to do?" Santa rubs his chin in a circular motion, "Well, I was wondering if you knew anything about the reindeer?" Madison replies in a fast flick of the tongue, "No, I am sorry. I don't." Santa nods in an understanding manner, "Hmm. You did not happen to see anyone come in here last night. Did you, Madison?" Madison looks towards the ground sharply, "Uh, no." Santa inhales deeply, "Okay, well if you are sure." Madison speaks in a smooth tone, "How will you ever find out what hurt the reindeer?" Santa shoots her a fast wink, "I always find out the truth." Santa groans, "Madison, I have a lot to do before tonight and I cannot do my job if he is sick. He is my lead reindeer and without him, Christmas will just not happen this year. So, I am leaving it up to you and Alex to figure out what is wrong with him and get it fixed." Madison turns towards Alex, "How are you ever going to figure out what is wrong with him and fix it before tonight?" Alex shrugs, "I do not know." Madison huffs, "If only we could talk to him and ask him what was wrong, this would be a lot easier." Alex knocks his head back, "I know, but to be able to do that we would need a Christmas miracle." Madison can feel tears beginning to roll down her cheeks. Alex has a hint of fear lining his tone, "What is the matter? Please, do not cry." Madison's voice cracks loudly, "How will I ever be able to save my grandmother, now? Without the reindeer, Santa will have no way to get to Star Dust Peak."

Madison wipes the tears away from her eyes, "Alex, I have to tell you something, but you cannot tell anyone." Alex nods once in understanding, "Okay, you can tell me anything. What is the matter?" Madison huffs, "Uh. Well, you see I kind of, sort of snuck out of the office last night, when you told me not to. I came in here by the reindeer and some of my fairy dust got on him. I did not tell anyone, because I did not want you or Santa to be mad at me." Alex throws his head back, "That is it! Magic on magic! Something happened when your magic touched his. We have to get him fixed. Anything can happen when magic meets magic." Madison feels hopeful, "Okay, what do we do?" Alex smiles widely, "Find the spell book, follow me." Madison trails behind Alex as he leads her further back in the stables. Madison looks around at the surroundings, "Why would the book be here with the reindeer?" Alex smiles, "You do not know, Santa. The book could be anywhere."

Madison inhales deeply, "Why does it smell like cinnamon?" Alex laughs, "That is reindeer poop, see?" He points to three elves cleaning the stables to their right as they pass by. Madison finds this part of the North Pole to be interesting, she notices that there are baby reindeer trying to learn how to fly in their stables to the left. Their wobbly legs are causing them to run into their mother. Madison cannot help but to giggle in response. Alex looks over his shoulder, "They are reindeer in training." Madison smiles brightly, "I think they need a little work." Alex keeps talking to Madison, but all she can hear is what sounds like words all mumbled together as her mind is distracted by something else. When Madison does not answer, Alex stops causing her to fly right into his back. He speaks in a harsh tone, "Madison!" The boom of his voice pulls her free from her daze causing her to blink rapidly, "Sorry, Alex. I cannot stop thinking about the baby reindeer. I want one so bad, they are just so cute! Can we at least go back so I can pet them?" Alex shoots back sharply, "No! You cannot touch them. You have seen what happened to one reindeer. We do not need the babies sick, too!" Madison huffs, "I guess, you are right."

Now that they have ventured through the entire stable area, Alex speaks in a disappointed tone, "Well, we did not find anything here. So, I guess it is time to look somewhere else." Madison squints sharply, "Where to now?" Alex exhales loudly, "How about the elves' kitchen?" Madison's voice cracks in response, "What is that?" Alex smiles widely, "Come on, I will show you!"

Alex leads Madison out back to where the elves are working on toys. They seem to be dressed the same as Alex, except they have on chef hats and aprons. The aroma of smells mixing inside of her nose causes her to sneeze repeatedly. Alex laughs, "Does your family cook a lot at home?" Madison drops her head, "No, not really. This is all new to me." Alex smiles, "Well, while I am checking out the room for the book, why don't you go around and watch the elves." Madison frowns, "But, I could help you and the faster we find the book, the better." Alex shrugs in a careless sway, "Well, it is not every day that you wind up in Santa's workshop, either. Go have fun. I will come find you when the search is through and I am ready to search another area." Madison smiles while nodding her head in agreement.

41

Madison is nervous at first as she flies up behind one elf. She is not sure what to expect, but she tries to see over her shoulder, wondering what it is that she is doing, but Madison soon finds that her hat keeps getting in the way. The elf spins around quickly in order to do something, almost knocking Madison out of the air. She screams in desperation, "Look out!"

The elf completely freezes in response, "Who said that?"

Madison flies right in front of her face, "I did. I am Madison. I am helping Santa and Alex. What are you making?"

The elf smiles widely, "Candy canes. Would you like to try one?"

Madison nods her head yes and to her surprise, the elf cuts out a tiny piece of the material.

She hands it to Madison, who immediately notices that it is a very sticky substance. She passes it back and forth in between her hands, the smell of peppermint is so strong it is making her eyes water. She slowly raises the candy to her mouth, closing her eyes expecting the worst. Once the candy cane hits her tongue, it slowly begins to melt in her mouth. Madison opens her eyes widely as a smile slowly creeps onto her face, "I love it!" The elf cannot help but to release a fit of laughter.

Madison ventures to the next table, where she finds that the elves are making something that looks like a house. Madison flies up next to it, trying to get a better look inside when an elf asks, "Would you like to try our gingerbread house?" Madison does not even have a chance to answer before she notices that her vision is flooded with a large piece of cookie being pushed towards her, urging her to take it. The weight of the cookie nearly brings her down with it as she grabs it the best she can. The dough is warm inside of her grasp causing her palms to sweat, the action grosses her out as she thinks, *'I wonder if he would give me another piece?'* She finds that she is too shy to ask, so she comes to the conclusion, *'If I just eat it fast and I do not think about it I will have nothing to worry about.'* Madison smells a strong hint of cinnamon coming from the dough as she slides as much of the cookie as she can into her mouth. Her face turns sour as she hurries over to the trash can to spit it out. The elf who handed her the cookie rushes over to her side, "What is the matter? Do you not like it?" Madison gives him a nervous smile, "I guess, everyone has different tastes." The elf leads her towards another table, "Maybe, you will like what they are making over here." He smiles gently before going back to his original station.

Madison looks at the new table, to see they are making the same kind of cookies that Mrs. Claus had given her the night before. Madison decides to play when the nearest elf hands her a piece of cookie to taste as if she had never had it before. With the warm, gooey cookie in her hand she has no hesitation while scarfing down the bite. The elf looks surprised, "It looks as though you did not even get to taste it, you ate it so fast. Would you like another piece?" Madison nods her head yes as the elf hands her more cookie crumbs.

She begins to put one of the bites in her mouth, when the noise of the workshop is broke by Alex yelling, "Madison! Where are you?" Madison puts the cookie crumbs inside of the pocket on her dress, figuring that she can just save them for later. Madison flies over to Alex in a quick swoop, "What is the matter? Did you find the book?" Alex shakes his head, "No, I did not. I just wanted to find you, so we could move on to the next place. How did you like the elves' kitchen?" Madison smiles, "I loved it! Where to now? Somewhere with more food, I hope!" Alex laughs, "Actually, you are going to have to get inside of my shirt pocket again to stay warm. We are heading back outside." Madison seems shocked, "Outside? Why outside?" Alex shrugs, "Well, there is really nowhere else to look inside of here. The next place is the village. I think you will like it."

Alex places Madison inside of his shirt pocket as he takes the first few steps outside. They are hit hard by a chilly burst of wind.

Alex speaks in an attempt to distract her from the weather conditions, "It is late, everything in the village is already closed. We will have to go store by store and look inside of the windows, to see if we spot the book hidden anywhere. It is our only option, right now. This is the busiest season of the year. All of the elves are pitching in to help Santa."

Madison cuddles up as close as she can to Alex as she nods her head in agreement as they begin walking down the sidewalk of the village.

Madison is in complete awe of all of the decorations. The street lights are wrapped in bulbs of color and garland. The buildings are lined with white, sparkling stars and gigantic bows that are hanging above each window. Wooden, candy cane figures are nailed to the side of every building. The sidewalks are lined with red and white lights as they are entangled in between each snow drift, guiding their way. In the middle of the town, stands a huge Christmas tree. It is fully decorated in ornaments of all sizes, garland, tinsel, lights of all colors, popcorn and even cookies. They hover above what looks like a million gifts piled around the tree. Madison's imagination begins to wonder what each one might hold inside and how badly she wants each and every single one. Her daydreaming is cut short by Alex, "This is where they make all of our shoes."

Alex places her on the ground beside his leg as they press their faces against the window, looking inside to see a dull and dark room. Shelves are filled to the ceiling of shoes ranging in all of the colors you could possibly think of. Madison looks down at her feet, "Do you think they make any that would fit me?" Alex smirks slightly, "I do not think he could work on a project so small, I am sorry." Madison laughs wholeheartedly, "It is okay, I can always just admire yours."

Alex nudges her right shoulder slightly, convincing her that they need to move on to the next building. Madison looks inside, "What is this?" Alex tips his head towards the window, "Where we buy all of our clothes." Madison presses her face as hard as she can to the glass surface trying to get a good look. When she removes her facial structure from the window, red marks line her forehead, "They are all the same." Alex nods his head once, "Yes, I know. For some reason, Santa thinks it is best for all of us to look the same, so no one can say they are better or less than anyone else. Santa thinks that it will keep us elves happier." Madison appears to allow his words to fully sink in, "I can see how that makes sense."

Madison points to the next building with excitement, "Oh, what is that?" Alex walks over to the structure, "That is the hospital. It is where all of the elves were born, including myself." Madison squints her eyes sharply, "All of you?" Alex nods, "Yes. We have not had an elf born at the North Pole for some time now." Madison pushes her lips into a slight frown, "How long has it been?" Alex rolls his eyes back, "Almost a hundred years." Madison's eyes widen, "Wow! That is a long time. Do you think that since no one has been born in so long that Santa might have hidden the book in here?"

Alex smirks, "It is a possibility, but there are still Nurses and Doctors in here daily, just in case any of us get sick."

They look through the windows, but they are heavily tinted. Madison throws the weight of her arms to her sides, "What are we supposed to do, now? We cannot see a thing!" Alex releases a deep breath of air, "If nothing else, we will come back later. If we cannot find it anywhere else." Madison nods her head in agreement as she points at the last building on that side of the street. Alex nods once to her curiosity, "Yes, yes. We are going there next, that is the bakery." Madison tilts her head, "The what?" Alex chuckles gently, "It is where the elves make donuts, pretzels, birthday cakes and sell hot chocolate." Madison licks her lips, "Why do you have the bakery, when you make so much candy and sweets inside of the workshop?" Alex shrugs, "Those are for the children to put inside of their stockings on Christmas Eve." Madison's bottom lip drops, "Do you think the book is in here?" Alex rolls his eyes in frustration, "I doubt it. The elf that runs this is not very friendly. I highly doubt Santa would ever come in here. The book has to be somewhere safe. It cannot fall into the wrong hands." Madison racks her mind, "Somewhere safe? Hmm, how about those houses?" Alex turns around to see where Madison is pointing, he laughs, "It would not be there, that is where all of the elves live. It would be way too risky to hide it there. Elves are constantly cleaning. If someone were to find it, it would ruin the North Pole and Christmas, if they use it without knowing how powerful it is. All of the secrets of the North Pole are inside of there." Madison pushes her eyebrows together, "Then how come Santa will not get mad if you use it?" Alex leans forwards slightly, "Listen, he will get mad, but I am one of three people, who know how to use it properly. Santa trusts me and he will never find out because we will have it back before he even notices it is gone, trust me." Madison feels guilty, but she knows she has to keep going. She sighs, "Where to next? Hopefully, somewhere inside because I am freezing." Alex frowns, "I am sorry to disappoint you. It is not inside. We have one more place to look, it is outside of the village." Madison throws her hands up, "Why would the book be in the middle of nowhere?" Alex shrugs, "Well, sometimes Santa goes on long walks outside of the village to clear his head and think, so maybe he has a secret storage room we do not know about." Madison is becoming anxious, "Well, can we please hurry? I am so cold." Alex chuckles, "Yes, I am sorry. We will hurry."

51

Madison and Alex are now trucking through the snow. Madison hides deep in his pocket, only allowing the top of her face to show. Alex uses his right hand to cover his eyes, trying to keep the wind out to prevent tears from piling up.

Madison yells up to him through the wind, "Do you see that thing in the distance?" Alex is really not paying attention to her as he wipes his eyes, "It Is probably just a cell tower." Madison grows excited, "Let's go check over there." Alex finds his feet carrying the weight of his body towards the object, Madison squeals, "Alex! That is not a tower! That is a huge bear!" Alex shakes his head in disbelief, "We do not have bears at the North Pole." He attempts to move closer, in order to get a better look. Madison hides shaken and scared inside of his pocket. Alex stops in front of the bear, he pokes his pocket, "It is okay, you can come out now. It is not going to hurt you. It is fake." Madison pops her tiny head in an upwards movement to see a twelve-foot, fluffy, brown, teddy bear sitting all alone in the snow. Madison peers up at Alex, "What is a fake bear doing all the way out here?" Before Alex has a chance to answer, the bear speaks in a deep growl, "Who are you calling fake? What are you doing here? State your reason for being here." Alex can feel shaken words flooding his mouth, "Um. I am Alex, Santa's right-hand man. We are looking for a book." The bear wastes no time to get to the point, "What kind of book do you seek?" Alex attempts to sound brave, "A spell book, but Santa cannot know we were here." The bear presents an item, "This book?" He holds up a black covered book, with a bright white light shining around it, nearly blinding Madison and Alex. Alex covers his eyes with his right hand, "Yes, sir. That is the book." The bear puts the book back away, "Payment." Alex squints, "What?" The bear again states firmly, "Payment. In order to get the book, one must pay me first." Alex takes a step forward, "Pay you in what?" The bear roars, "Figure it out."

SPELL BOOK

Madison flies up in front of the bear's face, reaching her right hand into the pocket of her dress, pulling out the cookie crumbs along with small pieces of leaves that had fallen off of her dress. She holds them up to his face. The bear stares down at Madison and her tiny crumbs. The bear laughs a powerful howl, "What am I supposed to do with that?" Madison's voice shakes, "Uh. Well, it is very good and I thought that you could eat it. Do you not like cookies?" The bear scuffs, "I like cookies, not crumbs. Those would only get stuck in my teeth. So, no book!" Madison puts her head down and flies back by Alex, "What are we going to do now? The cookie was all I had." Alex begins to panic, "Maybe, we could sing him a song." Madison's eyes widen, "What kind of song?" Alex scans the area around them looking for a theme, "Well, a Christmas song!" Madison's voice breaks, "I do not know any Christmas songs!" Alex strains his neck sharply, "Then make one up. I will follow your lead." Madison takes a deep breath, "I am a fairy, who flew to the North Pole in search of Santa and now I am face to face with a big, scary bear." Alex looks at Madison with fear, "That does not even sound like a song!" The bear demands, "Silence! I hate music! No more singing!" Madison turns towards Alex, "Great, now what?" Alex shifts his focus onto the bear, "I do not know. What would you like to receive as payment?"

Madison thinks for a moment, "I got an idea!" She flies up to the bear's face and lands upon his nose. She then hugs it super tight, but before letting go, she gives it a kiss. She hurries and zooms back down to Alex, not knowing how the bear is going to react.

The bear blushes a deep red, before releasing a hardy laugh while handing the book to Alex.

Alex flushes with anger, "That was it? A hug!"

The bear glares at him, "Sometimes the greatest gift is love."

Madison giggles.

Alex shakes his head in irritation, "Come on, Madison. Let's go back to the workshop. I am freezing my ears off."

Madison hops back inside of Alex's shirt pocket, then to her relief realizes things were starting to go her way.

Madison speaks in a shivering hum, "So, now what do we do?"

Alex is still steaming from their earlier encounter with the bear, "Go back to the workshop, go into the stables and do a spell on the reindeer. Then I will bring the book back to the bear and everything is fixed."

They walk into the workshop, passing all of the elves back towards the stables. Madison and Alex are shocked to see that Santa is standing outside of the stable.

Madison panics, "Alex, what do we do now?"

Alex's face drains of all color, "I honestly have no idea."

They get up close to Santa, when he looks at them in disappointment, "Unless we know what is causing him to be sick, there is nothing we can do to save Christmas. No spell or magic can save him without a cause to his sickness."

Madison begins to feel guilty. She takes a deep breath and flies out of Alex's pocket allowing herself to land softly upon Santa's shoulder, "I am so sorry, I flew into the reindeer's cage and some of my fairy dust got onto him. I told Alex what had happened and we went to find the book of spells to help him. We finally found it but I guess, it does not matter now. You said it yourself, *Nothing can help the reindeer.* I am sorry I lied to you. I just did not want you to be angry. I guess, this means you are not going to help me save my grandmother, huh?"

Santa throws his head back while laughing, "Of course, I am still going to help you. I know you came in here by my reindeer. I knew the whole time. I was simply waiting for you to come tell me yourself."

Santa then reaches into his coat pocket to retrieve a blue, velvet bag.

He grabs some dust out of the bag, sprinkling it on the reindeer, who begins to float into the air. He is gently placed on the now sturdy structure of his hoofs, before he immediately takes off in a wobbly run towards his food to ease the rumbling of his stomach.

Alex's mouth drops open, "What! How did you do that without the book?"

Santa frowns down on him, "You never needed the book."

Alex throws his arms up in defeat, "But, Madison and I went through all of that trouble to get it!"

Santa crosses his arms over his chest, "I know, but that is exactly why both of you should have come and told me, first! Now, that my lead reindeer is fixed, we have a Christmas to get started!"

Santa reaches down, retrieving Madison from the stable floor, placing her on his shoulder as they start heading towards the sleigh.

Alex is still standing in front of the stable with his mouth wide open, holding onto the book.

Santa notices Alex is not following, so he yells back, "Are you coming or not? We will leave without you!"

Alex slowly begins walking after them, dragging the book against the ground in defeat. Now, that they are all inside of the sleigh, they begin waving goodbye to Mrs. Claus and the elves.

Santa yells, "Come on, boys you know what to do!"

The sleigh begins to shake and rattle as the front lifts off the ground.

Madison whispers, "Goodbye."

The word is released from under her breath as they fly out of the North Pole. The motions of the ride make Madison feel sleepy. She tucks herself once again inside of Alex's shirt pocket falling asleep.

Before she knows what is happening, she hears the deep boom of a man's voice, "Madison, wake up. You are home."

Madison allows her eyes to flutter, seeing the blurred image of her home bleeding into her mind. She awakens and jumps out of the sleigh, running inside of her house. She uses both of her fists to pound on her father's bedroom door.

He awakes with a startle, "Madison, what is it? What is the matter?"

She grabs him firmly by the hand and drags him outside, "Look, Daddy, look! It is him! It is Santa! I told you he was real!"

Her father's eyes shine with a light that Madison has never seen in them before. He just stands there blankly staring at Santa and his reindeer.

Santa laughs while speaking to her father, "Are you just going to stand there and stare at me all day? We have decorations to put up!"

Santa points to the huge tree in the center of Star Dust Peak as he throws her father a bundle of garland, "We have Christmas to set up for."

Her father smiles slightly. Santa and him begin to decorate the trees. While they are working hard on that, Alex and Madison are going to every house to hang a stocking upon each door for the kids inside.

Once they are all finished Santa speaks breathlessly, "I must go, now. I have had a long night and I am wanted at home."

Madison hugs them before they get into the sleigh.

Madison runs over to her father and greets him with a huge, warm hug while whispering in his ear, "Does this mean Grandma can stay?" Her father smiles and nods his head yes. Madison turns towards Santa, hoping he would still be there as she yells out for him, "Thank you for saving my grandmother!" He smiles and waves, yelling back to Madison, "No, thank you for saving Christmas!" While they fly off into the sky. Madison and her father are staring silently at the decorations with his arm around her shoulders. Her father breaks the silence when he kneels down on one knee, "I am sorry, for telling you that you have to be the same as everyone else. You need to be yourself and you have every right to believe in what you want." Madison's heart feels warm as she hugs her father tight. He speaks softly, "We have to go to sleep. It is so late and past your bed time!" Her father chases her inside of the house and playfully tosses her onto her bed. She crawls under the covers as he tucks her in and kisses her forehead. While he is walking out the door she whispers, "Merry Christmas." He turns out the light as he slowly shuts the door whispering back, "Merry Christmas, Madison."

The next morning, Madison wakes up with a fast jolt. At first, forgetting where she was. When she realizes she is in her own bed, her heart begins to hurt as she thinks to herself, *'It was only a dream.'* She slowly walks to the window, with her head hung down low. The sound of children laughing catches her attention from outside. She looks up and sees the tree, the lights and decorations which are all still there. She runs through the house yelling, "It's Christmas! It's Christmas! Everyone, wake up!" She runs outside and not too long after is joined by her father, mother and grandmother, who are standing behind her taking in the view. Her grandmother asks, "Do you know what would make this Christmas perfect?" Madison looks up at her, "What is that?" Her grandmother replies, "Snow." The second the words leave her mouth, a snowflake falls down and lands on Madison's nose. She looks up to see more beginning to fall. In the sky, way up high, she sees Santa flying above her house. She waves and sees him wave back. She smiles as her father kisses her on the head, "Thank you for bringing magic back into my heart."

# THE END

*The young fairy mother shuts the book and kisses her daughter on the head, "That my child, is the story of how I started Christmas in Star Dust Peak."*